LEGO NINJAGO
Masters of Spinjitzu

Arthur Braidwood

 Ladybird

Published by Ladybird Books Ltd 2011

A Penguin Company
Penguin Books Ltd, 80 Strand, London, WC2R 0RL, UK
Penguin Books Australia Ltd, Camberwell, Victoria, Australia
Penguin Group (NZ), 67 Apollo Drive, Rosedale, Auckland
0632, New Zealand (a division of Pearson New Zealand Ltd)

"The Master of Fire", "In His Footsteps",
"The Master of Ice" and "Getting the Joke"
written by Greg Farshtey

LEGO, the LEGO logo, the Brick and Knob configurations and the Minifigure
are trademarks of the LEGO Group.
©2011 The LEGO Group.
 Produced by AMEET Sp. z o.o.
under license from the LEGO Group.

Distributed by Penguin Books Ltd, 80 Strand, London, WC2R 0RL, UK
Please keep the Penguin Books Ltd address for future reference.

ISBN: 9781409310334
001 - 10 9 8 7 6 5 4 3 2 1
Printed in Poland

Contents

The Four Ninjas

When Sensei Wu's evil brother, Lord Garmadon, threatened the peace of Ninjago, the Sensei went searching for four special boys – those who would have the ability to become ninjas. Garmadon wanted to steal the four powerful golden Weapons of Spinjitzu, and the Sensei needed the ninjas to help stop him. These four ninjas would need to harness an amazing power – the art of Spinjitzu – in order to fight Garmadon and his skeleton army. In this book, find out why the Sensei chose Kai and Zane, and learn how you too can learn the art of the ninjas...

Meet Kai ● ● ●

Kai could have made a good blacksmith, had he only been half as patient as his father. When his sister was kidnapped by Garmadon's skeletons, Kai agreed to learn from Sensei Wu, for only with ninja skills could he hope to free her. Wu had a bigger plan for him, though, and soon the humble black-smith turned into a Master of Spinjitzu!

Personality:
Quick to anger and even quicker to act; loves music and breakdancing

Element:
Fire

Skills:
Very agile – a key skill for a Spinjitzu Master!

Weapon:
Swords, especially the most powerful of all – the Dragon Sword of Fire!

... and Nya

Nya ran the blacksmith shop with her brother. She is kind and gentle, but when the evil Lord Garmadon's army attacked she proved she was no easy victim. She fought five skeletons at once (and enjoyed it!) – until she was kidnapped by the enemy.

The Master of Fire

Of the four young men I recruited to join my fight against Garmadon, easily the most...challenging was Kai. He was the last of the group and my hope was that he would become the Ninja of Fire. Certainly his temperament made him ideal for that element.

Kai is the son of one of my oldest and most trusted friends. He and his sister Nya were raised by their father. They lived in a little village, far from any major city, a place where one could work and strive for years and never be known of by anyone beyond your settlement. Kai's father worked as a blacksmith and Kai was his apprentice.

Training Kai in the art of forging weapons and armour was, I gather, not an easy task, for the same reason it was not easy to train him to be a ninja. He is impatient, reckless, quick to anger, and reluctant to listen to the advice of others. His manner can be brash, but I believe that is a shield he has built against the world. With the passing of his father, Kai became the man of the family with the responsibility to look after his sister. That can be a great burden for a youth.

I found Kai and Nya at work in their shop, 4 Weapons. Unfortunately, Samukai and his skeleton warriors arrived at the same time, in search of a map that marked the locations of the Four Weapons of Spinjitzu.

The skeletons attacked, and in the battle, made off with both the map and Nya. I convinced Kai that by accepting my training, he would have the best chance to retrieve his sister safely.

With the help of my other three young warriors, I set about teaching him what I could of the art of battle. It was not easy.

The challenge was how to break him of his bad habits – rash actions, dangerous risk-taking, and letting his emotions cloud his thoughts – without breaking his spirit. The other three, Cole, Jay, and Zane, had had more time together and knew how to work as a team. Kai was used to being on his own, except for Nya, and was reluctant to rely on others.

Ah, Nya . . . I do not know why Garmadon ordered the young girl's capture, except perhaps to use as a hostage against me in the future. Its most immediate effect was on Kai. He was consumed with the desire to rescue her, which blinded him to almost everything else. I feared that in the heat of battle he would put himself or the others in danger out of concern for Nya.

Still, there was much potential in Kai, potential I am happy to say was realised.

He is brave, loyal, intelligent and willing to work hard to better himself. He has speed and grace, two key ingredients in mastering Spinjitzu. He is also fearless. I have no doubt he would challenge Garmadon himself in single combat if given half a chance, and never feel a moment's hesitation.

I look at Kai and I see his father. They share the same tendency to rush headlong into danger, and the same passion for life and devotion to family. Even some of Kai's moves in mock combat echo his father's. Kai did not know of his father's past, thinking of him only as a simple blacksmith, until I told him.

In the end, I am happy to say that Kai justified my faith in him. He earned the Dragon Sword of Fire he wields now. More importantly, he learned to work as part of a team and to see the grand picture of the world rather than focusing on just his corner of it. He could have left with Nya and returned to his village and his old life, and no one would have thought less of him for it. But he chose to stand beside his partners and prepare for any future danger that might threaten.

Does he still leap into danger? Yes. Is he still both amazing and exasperating? Yes. Is he like the fire he wields, burning hot and bright, no matter what? Yes, indeed. He is Kai, unique as a spark of flame, sharp as the sword he carries, a true hero at last.

The Sword and its Master

The most famous Japanese sword is the katana. It has a slightly curved, slender, single-edged blade, a circular or square guard, and a long grip to accommodate two hands.

Sword-smiths used up to five pieces of different types of steel to forge the katana. Heating and hammering took several days, while polishing took up to three weeks! Only then did the blade gain its perfect mirror finish and unique sharpness.

Due to this long and complex process, the katana was an expensive weapon. The highest-class katanas were called "meitou", meaning "celebrated sword" or "named sword". They were prized swords passed through generations of samurai, won in battle, or given as a gift out of respect.

The first Master of Spinjitzu used the power of the Dragon Sword of Fire to create Ninjago. Today the sword has a new master – Kai.

Ninja World: Weapons

In the skilled hands of a ninja even a simple stick can be useful. Do you know the ninjas' favourite weapons?

Nunchucks

A weapon consisting of two sticks connected at the ends with a short chain or rope. They were probably developed from a farming tool.

Bo staff

A long staff made of tapered hard wood, such as white oak or bamboo. Originally it was used for carrying baskets or buckets at its ends.

Shuriken

A star-shaped sharpened blade or a knife used for throwing, small enough to be concealed in the hand. Often covered with poison.

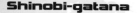

Shinobi-gatana

A sword with a katana-length grip, a square guard and a short straight blade that enabled it to be drawn quickly. Known also as ninjato.

Shuko

Metal bands with four curved spikes on one side. Ninjas fit them over their hands to climb trees, scale walls, or to parry sword attacks.

Kyoketsu-shoge

A long rope or a chain with an L-shaped double-edged blade at one end and a big metal ring at the other. Also used as a climbing tool.

The Sensei asks

Many things are not what they seem in the ninja world. One weapon described here was a creation of myth-makers and did not really exist. Which one?

Answer: Shinobi-gatana. There is no historical evidence of such a sword. It was probably invented by Hollywood film-makers.

The Way of the Ninjas: First Steps

One who wishes to become a ninja must be prepared for continual challenges. Let me guide you through the first steps on the way of the ninjas.

Step 1

Being a ninja is not about fighting enemies physically, but about fighting and overcoming your own weaknesses and fear.

Step 2

Write a list of your goals, and plan how much time you need to achieve them. Mark your achievements regularly, so you know if you are making any progress.

Step 3

Start learning any one of the martial arts. They are a great way of keeping your body agile and flexible. It is important to learn from a trained instructor or at a good school.

Step 4

Develop your body through regular exercise, swim a lot, and try adventure activities like rock-climbing. Good stamina and a fit body are key factors for ninja training.

Step 5

Exercise your mind with games like chess and mathematical problems. Only with a trained mind can you quickly plan the best strategy at the moment you need it.

Step 6

Learn to be patient. It takes years of practice, training and discipline to become a true ninja warrior. You can start by meditating — it will help your body, mind and soul to relax.

Sensei asks

Healthy food keeps the body healthy. Which food does not fit in the ninja diet: brown rice, sesame seeds, buckwheat, pizza, tofu, fish, or vegetables?

Answer: Pizza is delicious, but it is not really healthy food. A true ninja would have some fruit instead.

In His Footsteps

Kai crouched down, his brow knitted in concentration. His eyes were locked on the practice dummy ten feet away. It was just a thing of cloth and sticks, but it seemed to be making fun of him. He could almost hear it saying, "Ha! You call that a flying kick? You look like a chicken trying to fly...with one wing...blindfolded."

The young would-be ninja broke into a run. On his fifth stride, he planted his right foot and leaped into the air. His left foot was pointed straight out before him and aimed right at the target dummy's head. This time, Kai would knock the head off. He was sure of it.

Just short of contact, he faltered. His left leg dropped perhaps half an inch, just enough to throw off his balance. He fought to correct it, but that only made the problem worse. Suddenly, his flying kick had turned into a confused jumble, arms and legs going every which way. Kai landed on his rear end, bounced, rolled, and ended up at the foot of the practice dummy.

Nearby, Sensei Wu looked on. After a moment, he began to slowly clap his hands. "Amazing," he said. "Not just anyone can botch a flying kick that badly. That takes real talent."

Kai got to his feet, brushing the dirt off his clothes. That had been his twelfth attempt at the manoeuvre and his twelfth failure. He was angry at himself. His sister, Nya, was missing, captured by skeleton warriors, and she needed him to save her. And here he was struggling to master the battle techniques he would need to know, while time was perhaps running out for her.

For the first time, he began to doubt himself. What if Sensei Wu had been wrong to choose him for training? What if he didn't have what it took to be a ninja, or to learn the art of Spinjitzu? Maybe he was just a blacksmith, as his father had been. Was he fooling himself that he could ever become a warrior?

"Try it again," repeated Sensei Wu, sipping from his cup of tea. Kai had never seen him actually make any tea, but he always seemed to have a cup of it in his hand.

"What's the use?" Kai answered, his eyes on the ground. "Maybe I'm not cut out for this. Maybe I should go back to making swords and armour."

Sensei Wu smiled, remembering the incredibly bad sword he had seen Kai forge. "Yes, as I recall, you were a master at that."

Kai shot him a hard look. "Okay, so maybe my work was a little...creative. At least I knew which end of the sword to put in the fire. Here? I'm not a ninja. I work in a blacksmith shop in a market square, just like my father did. I've lived in that village my whole life, the same as he did. We're just regular people. We're not warriors and adventurers."

Sensei Wu gently eased himself down onto a chair. He was looking in Kai's direction, but his eyes were focused on a past time. When he spoke, it was very quietly.

"Your father," Sensei Wu said, "did not live in that village all his life."

"What are you talking about?" asked Kai. "You told me that when you decided to hide the Four Weapons of Spinjitzu from your evil brother, you came to our village. You asked my father to draw a map showing the locations of the four hiding places."

"True," said Sensei Wu. "And from that day to this, I had never set foot in your village again...because your father asked me not to."

Kai looked at the Sensei in disbelief. "That's crazy. You're a Sensei, a master of Spinjitzu, and you let a blacksmith tell you where you could and couldn't go?"

"No," Sensei Wu answered. "I respected the wishes of my best friend."

Seeing the expression on Kai's face, Sensei Wu smiled softly. "You look surprised. Did you not think Spinjitzu masters had friends? There was a time when your father and I travelled the length of this land, righting wrongs and aiding the weak. That was long before you were born, of course, or your sister."

"Are you saying my father knew Spinjitzu?"

Sensei Wu shook his head. "No. He could have, if he had chosen that path. But he did not."

There was an uncomfortable silence. Finally, Kai sat down at Sensei Wu's feet and said, "I never knew any of this. Tell me about him...please."

"Your father was wise, brave, and the most trusted ally any man could have," Sensei Wu began.

"We fought together for many years, sometimes even with Garmadon beside us, before my brother turned bad. We brought peace where there had been disorder. Your father was a hero, Kai."

The Sensei smiled. "In the early days, he was much like you – headstrong, reckless. Once, we were searching for a group of samurai bandits. Your father was sure he saw them in a nearby field

in the moonlight. Without waiting for me, he drew his sword and charged."

"What happened?" asked Kai.

"In the morning, we had to pay the farmer for all the scarecrows your father had 'defeated'," the Sensei said, with a chuckle.

"As time passed, Garmadon and I grew further apart. I came to rely on your father's advice and aid more and more. Yet another life beckoned to him. He had met and married the woman who would be your mother. Eventually, you and Nya were born. He chose to lay down his sword, settle in this village, and be with his family."

"Why?" asked Kai. "Why would he choose to live in a little out-of-the-way place when he had a life full of adventure?"

"I asked the same question, at the time," answered Sensei Wu. "Your father's answer was, 'Protecting the world begins with protecting the ones you love. There are many men who can wield a sword or win a battle. But only I can be a husband to my wife and a father to Kai and Nya.'"

Kai shrugged. It still didn't make sense to him. "And that was it? You two said goodbye?"

Sensei Wu nodded. "For a very long time, yes – where I travelled, danger travelled with me, and your father did not want his children put in jeopardy. When I finally defeated Garmadon and chose to hide the weapons of Spinjitzu, I knew I had to share the secret of their location with someone I trusted."

"So you came to my father," said Kai.

"He made the map and hid it where we hoped no one would find it – inside the banner of your shop,"

Sensei Wu replied. "He knew it was a risk, keeping it here, but it was a greater one to allow it out of his sight. And I slept peacefully, knowing it was in his care."

"But Garmadon found it anyway."

Sensei Wu nodded. Kai said nothing for a long time. Finally, he looked up and asked, "Do you think my father would be proud of me?"

"If you try again, yes," Sensei Wu replied. "If you quit...that he would not understand. Your father chose to be a different kind of hero, a kind I could never be. He knew he was the only one who could raise you and Nya and keep you strong and safe. And, Kai, you are the only one who can do what needs to be done now."

Kai stood and walked back to his start position. Once again, he concentrated on the training dummy. He pictured every movement he would make, from his leap to sailing straight and true through the air towards the target. But this time, as he began to run, he felt something more than a determination to succeed. He knew he was running in the footsteps of his father.

I will learn everything Sensei Wu can teach me, Kai thought, as he took off into the air. *I will rescue Nya, father. I will carry on your legacy and make you proud.*

There was no confusion, no wasted motion, now — simply a young man with fire in his heart doing what he must do. He was one with his body and the world around him seemed to slow down. Then his left foot landed on the target dummy, punching through the straw and sticks and rags. The dummy toppled as Kai landed cleanly on his feet.

Sensei Wu gave the barest of smiles. "Better. Today, you fought your first great enemy – your own doubts – and you won. Take that victory into your tomorrows and you will bring honour to your name...and to the memory of your father."

"Phew!" said Kai. "After all that, I'm thirsty. Got any more of that tea?"

Sensei Wu smiled. "Snatch the cup from my hand without disturbing the tea inside...and we'll talk."

The Menace to Ninjago

Sensei Wu defeated his evil brother, Lord Garmadon, and banished him to live in the Underworld. He had long dreamed of returning to Ninjago – he was master of the Power of Destruction, but he envied Wu's Power of Creation. The desire to control the elements and rebuild the world in his own image drove him mad. So, he allied with the Underworld's dark forces – Samukai and his skeleton army – who helped to steal the Four Weapons of Spinjitzu. Garmadon used the weapons to escape the Underworld, but the amazing ninjas thwarted his wicked plan.

The Fire Dragon

The mighty Fire Dragon guarded one of the Four Golden Weapons of Spinjitzu – the Dragon Sword of Fire – hidden in the Temple of Fire. Kai's first meeting with the dragon was, obviously, far from pleasant.

Garmadon lured Kai to the temple and, by threatening Nya, forced him to get the sword for him. My intervention saved both Kai and Nya from Garmadon, but then the dragon sealed off our escape.

The Fire Dragon unleashed his wrath against Kai and Nya, as I disappeared into the Underworld with the sword. Once it realised they were trying to protect the sword, the dragon turned out to be quite friendly.

Legends about dragons say that these mystical creatures belonged to both Ninjago and the Underworld, and shuttled back and forth between them. Kai worked out that the great beast was his chance to follow me to the Underworld.

Oriental Dragons

For centuries people have both feared and admired dragons. Here's a fistful of myths and facts about oriental dragons.

1. The dragon is a powerful symbol of creative and active forces. It has always been present in the art and architecture of the East. It is also seen as a symbol of success and prosperity.

2. Japanese dragons, called "tatsus", are large, snake-like beasts with scaly bodies that live in lakes and springs. If annoyed, they are likely to cause great floods, rather than breathing fire.

3. Oriental dragons can fly, even though usually they do not have wings. According to some legends dragons gained wings after living for at least a thousand years.

4. Japanese dragons have three toes on each foot. It is said that dragons grew toes as they travelled, and if they went too far they would end up with too many toes to be able to walk properly.

5. In Japanese legends, dragons could change size and shape. Many a story tells about a dragon turning into a human, or a human into a dragon. Dragons could even become invisible, if they wished.

6. Oriental dragons tended to be wise and benevolent – as long as they were given the respect they deserved. Their major flaw was their vanity, and they could easily be insulted.

The Sensei asks

The colours of oriental dragons symbolise parts of the world. Black is the symbol of the North, blue of the East and red of the West. What do white dragons symbolise?

Answer: The South.

Ninja Quiz

When a mission ends, ninjas waste no time – they practise and test their skills. So, test your memory with this quiz, now!

1. What was Zane doing when I first met him?
2. What is one of Zane's amazing abilities?
3. Why did Zane decide to become a ninja?
4. What is Zane's major flaw?
5. What does Zane know of his family?
6. What was Zane's night mission near the Caves of Despair?
7. Whom did Zane meet in the woods?
8. What did Zane do to trick the skeleton?
9. What is Zane's hairstyle like?
10. What is the Ice Master of Spinjitzu's weapon?

Answers:
1. Meditating underwater. 2. Withstanding extreme cold. 3. To learn new things. 4. No sense of humour. 5. Nothing. 6. Gather wood for a campfire. 7. Skeleton Kruncha. 8. He made him believe they never met. 9. Short. 10. The Shurikens of Ice.

Contents

Masters of Spinjitzu

I never doubted that Kai, Jay, Cole and Zane were the chosen ones. But it was a long time before they finally understood what it took to master Spinjitzu and the elemental powers of Fire, Lightning, Earth and Ice. Only then could these four ninjas act as a team and defeat the evil Lord Garmadon. Only then could they save Ninjago...

Meet Zane

Personality:

Serious and studious – but not much good at having fun

Element:

Ice

Skills:

Zane is very stealthy and has the amazing ability of sixth sense

Weapon:

The incredibly powerful golden Shurikens of Ice

Zane is always cool as ice, quiet and focused. He is the most mysterious of the young men who allied with Sensei Wu in his struggle against Garmadon. Even though he seems a bit different to the other ninjas, Zane is a vital member of the team, dedicated and precise in combat. Many times he proved he was the right choice for the Ninja of Ice. He is a seer with sixth sense, but his own past is a mystery even to himself. Zane is curious about everything the world has to offer, and he learns quickly. He hopes to learn more about himself too – but first he wants to help save Ninjago.

The Master of Ice

Ah, Zane . . . will I ever solve the mystery that surrounds him? More importantly, will he ever learn the answers to all his questions? Sometimes, I fear not.

I had first heard rumours some time ago about a youth in a northern province capable of withstanding extreme cold. At the time, my other duties kept me from seeking him out. When my brother, Garmadon, threatened to steal the Four Weapons of Spinjitzu, I was forced to seek out potential ninjas. This caused my path to finally cross that of Zane.

I found him in a most unusual place. He was sitting in an icy lake, meditating. On the shore, a crowd of villagers had gathered, all of them marvelling at how long Zane had managed to stay underwater. Anyone else would surely have surfaced after a few minutes due to lack of air or the freezing cold, but Zane seemed to be hardly bothered by either condition. He was, however, quite shocked to open his eyes and see me seated down there with him.

Zane was an orphan... or, rather, he thought he might be, but was not sure. As it turned out, he was a young man without a past. He said he had awakened

one day near his village with no memory of how he had got there or where he had been before. All he knew was his name. He made his way into the village and earned a living doing jobs for various people. The fact that Zane was able to do work outdoors in brutally cold conditions made him much valued, especially by those who preferred to stay indoors by the fire during snowstorms.

When I asked him about training to be a ninja, he was slow to say yes at first. As we talked, he realised that there were many secrets he could learn through this training. That was how I discovered that Zane loves to learn and is always trying to find out new things.

Zane is, in fact, possibly the smartest of my four ninjas. That is, if you measure how smart someone is only by what they have learned from books. Zane can tell you why the grass is green, how a flower grows,

what makes a babbling brook sound the way it does. But I have never known him to smell a flower, lie in the grass and look at the clouds, or relax by a brook. I have seen him study the structure of a snowflake, but I wonder if he sees the beauty in the fact that no two are alike?

My other ninjas – Jay, Cole and Kai – have certainly noticed that Zane is a bit different from them. They talk about how he has no sense of humour. He rarely smiles and never laughs, and he doesn't seem to even get the jokes the other young men tell. Although they like him and respect him, it is sometimes hard for them to feel close to Zane. There is something about him that just feels... unique, and no one can identify what it is.

Despite his dedication to his training and the mission, I know Zane is troubled by the questions about his past. He wants to know the answers, but perhaps he fears them as well. What if his parents are still alive and searching for him? Or what if they are bandits and would want him to use his skills for crime? What if the story of his early years holds the key to everything about him that seems so strange to others?

Still, he has shown me again and again that he was the right choice to be my Ninja of Ice. When he faces an enemy, he seeks out points of weakness and targets them. When he strikes, it is not out of anger or

fear. Even when faced with a mighty Ice Dragon, Zane does not panic. I have seen Kai let his love for his sister blind him to danger, and Jay's humour desert him in a moment of crisis. But Zane is ice.

What does the future hold for this most mysterious of ninjas? I do not know. I believe he hopes his adventures with Kai and the others will somehow lead him to answers about his past. I truly believe he would go to the ends of the world to find out who he really is – and I and my ninjas will stand beside him as he searches for clues to this greatest of mysteries.

Ninjitsu:
Being Invisible

Ninjas hide where no other can find cover. Ninjas enter heavily guarded places without being noticed. Ninjas can do all this because they know ninjitsu.

"Ninjitsu" means "the art of stealth" or "the art of endurance". It is a system of combat and survival techniques originally developed by warrior monks in medieval Japan.

Ninjitsu techniques reflect the ninjas' close connection to nature and their belief that every element has its own energy and spirit. Ninjitsu training unifies ninjas with the forces of nature.

The techniques of moving in secrecy and hiding are key skills for ninjas. They make them "invisible" and enable them to perform their secret spying missions.

"Innin" are ninjitsu techniques used for actions covertly carried out on the opponent's territory. The techniques used during direct battles are called "yonin".

 Ninjitsu training can also involve disguise, surprising escape techniques, clever methods of distracting opponents, and even some elementary medicine.

 Throughout history many different schools (ryu) have taught their unique versions of this martial arts system, but the name "ninjitsu" was not given to it until the middle of the 20th century.

A ninja in disguise

Ninja World: Combat Styles

A warrior with versatile skills is more likely to defeat any opponent. Therefore it is wise and very practical to learn more than one martial art.

Aikido

A system of self-defence performed by blending with the motion of the attacker and redirecting the force of the attack rather than opposing it head-on. It requires very little physical strength.

Bojitsu

Bojitsu means "the art of the staff". It is the martial art of using a wooden staff weapon called a "bo". The practitioners of bojitsu follow the philosophy that the bo is merely an "extension of one's limbs".

Karate

Karate, meaning "empty hand", is a traditional Japanese combat system of fighting methods involving kicks and punches. Today karate is practised for self-perfection, for self-defence and as a sport.

Jujitsu

A martial art and a method of close combat for defeating an armed and armoured opponent in which one uses no weapon. Jujitsu focuses on blocking, dodging, and striking or throwing the opponent.

Judo

A modern martial art and a combat sport involving throwing the opponent to the ground and immobilising him with a grappling manoeuvre. "Ju" means "gentle" or "flexible" and "do" means "way" or "path".

Kendo

"The way of the sword", Kendo, is a modern form of Japanese fencing based on kenjitsu – the traditional samurai art of swordsmanship. Kendo is taught as part of the school curriculum in Japan.

The Sensei asks

Martial arts have grown very popular in the present day. One of them is now a part of the modern Olympic Games. Which one?

Answer: Judo. It was recognised as an Olympic sport in 1964.

The Way of the Ninjas: Eighteen Skills

The ninjas' strength lies in their adaptability, their weapons and their training ... which consists of eighteen disciplines called "ninja juhachikei".

 Seishinteki kyoyo
Spiritual refinement

Taijitsu
Unarmed defensive combat

 Kenjitsu
Sword techniques

Bojitsu
Stick and staff techniques

 Sojitsu
Spear techniques

Naginatajitsu
Halberd techniques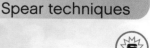

 Kusarigamajitsu
Sickle and chain techniques

Shurikenjitsu
Throwing weapons techniques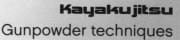

 Kayakujitsu
Gunpowder techniques

Hensojitsu
Disguise and impersonation

Shinobi-iri
Stealth Methods

Bajitsu
Horsemanship

Sui-ren
Water training

Boryaku
Strategy and tactics

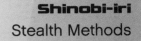

Choho
The art of espionage

Intonjitsu
Escaping and concealment

Tenmon
Using weather changes as a strategic weapon

Chimon
Knowledge of the surrounding area

The Sensei asks

Today, in schools all over the world, children learn a subject that belonged to ninja juhachikei. Can you guess what it is?

Getting the Joke

Zane picked his way carefully down the rocky hillside. His eyes had already adjusted to the darkness, but it would still have been easy to trip and fall. If he were to tumble and cry out, he might be warning Samukai's skeleton warriors that the ninjas were nearby. Worse, if he was badly injured, Sensei Wu and his three friends would have to leave him behind. The mission they were on was too dangerous and too important to risk its success.

The "mission" Zane was undertaking at the moment seemed far less important. Sensei Wu had sent him off to

gather sticks to build a fire. Although it was a cold evening in the mountains, Zane didn't see the sense in making a campfire. They were very close to the Caves of Despair, the place the Sensei was sure would be teeming with skeleton warriors. Why build a fire and potentially give away their position? Not for the first time, Zane wondered if the Sensei truly knew what he was doing.

The hillside suddenly grew much steeper. Zane found himself running faster than he wanted to towards the bottom, and only reaching out for a nearby tree slowed him. He glanced up and noticed that there were a number of branches that would make good firewood. As silently as possible, he began to climb the tree.

There could, of course, have been another good reason why the Sensei sent him off on this task. He had been travelling with the other ninjas – Cole, Jay, and Kai – for days now, but did not really fit in with them. Despite the danger they all were facing, the three youths were always laughing and joking. Zane never joined in. In fact, he couldn't remember ever really doing that. He had always been a serious person, devoted to meditation, and hadn't had time for humour and games.

The others didn't know that about him. All they saw was someone who didn't 'get' the joke. Maybe they were beginning to wonder if Zane was afraid of the challenges ahead of them and that was why he was so grim. If they had doubts about him, it might cause problems in battle.

Maybe the Sensei wanted time alone with the three to discuss this, so he sent Zane off on a pointless job.

Zane didn't think he was afraid. He certainly respected the power of Garmadon and Samukai – only a fool would not. But the feelings that came with fear – cold sweat, trembling, heart pounding – were absent from him. Much of what the ninjas would face was still unknown, and Zane saw no point in fearing the unknown. It was a waste of energy.

He was about to break off a small branch when he heard a twig snap down below. Flattening himself against the tree trunk, he waited and watched. In a few moments, he saw the moonlight gleaming off the polished bones of a skeleton warrior. The skeleton was alone and muttering to himself as he walked.

"Go get the wood, Kruncha," grumbled the skeleton. "Pick up those rocks, Kruncha. Stop eating all the doughnuts, Kruncha. Orders, orders, orders, that's all I ever hear."

Zane knew what he had to do. This Kruncha might stumble upon the camp and see Sensei Wu and the others. He would then rush back and report to Samukai. If the skeletons found out about the ninjas now, it would be a disaster. The success of the mission depended on surprise.

He waited until Kruncha was right under the tree. Then Zane let go of the trunk and jumped down on top of the skeleton. Kruncha let out an "oof" as Zane landed on him, and the two rolled around on the ground until they smacked into a big rock. Zane was stunned for an instant, allowing the skeleton to get to his bony feet.

"Ha!" said Kruncha. "You're my prisoner!"

Zane rolled aside and sprang into a crouch, a shuriken in his hand. "No. You are my prisoner."

"I said it first," insisted Kruncha.

"I hardly think that matters," Zane answered. "I have a shuriken. You dropped your sword 15.2 feet up the hill. How can I be your prisoner if you have no weapon?"

Kruncha smiled and tapped his head with a long finger of bone. "I have my brain ... well, actually, I don't really, but I'll bet I'm still smarter than you."

"Why would you think that?" asked Zane.

"For one thing, when I climb trees, I don't fall out of them," Kruncha said, with pride in his voice. "And I don't run around in the dark by myself in the middle of the night where I might run into trouble."

"Actually, I am pretty sure that is what you were doing when we met," Zane replied.

"Shows what you know," snapped Kruncha. "When you work for Samukai, you're never alone. Someone is always watching you to make sure you don't eat all the doughnuts."

Zane frowned. "How can you eat doughnuts when you have no stomach?"

Kruncha started to answer, then stopped, looking confused. A moment later, he opened his mouth again to speak, and stopped, seeming even more puzzled than before. He looked down at the ground and scratched his skull. Finally, he glared at Zane and said, "That's none of your business!"

"Turn around," said Zane. "I am taking you back to my friends."

Kruncha shook his head. "You turn around. Samukai will want to talk to you."

Zane threw his shuriken. It glanced off Kruncha's skull and ricocheted into the woods. The skeleton staggered for a second, but his bone was like armour so he wasn't harmed. Then the two began to fight furiously. First one was winning, then the other, but they were too evenly matched for either to win outright. They were rolling around on the grass when Kruncha hit his head on a rock and stopped fighting, dazed.

Zane got to his feet. *If I knew Spinjitzu, I could win, but I don't yet. We could fight all night, and if I lost, it would put the others in danger. Still, he's not too bright, so maybe...*

"You can't capture me," Zane said suddenly. "I'm not really here."

"Huh?" said Kruncha. "But you fell out of a tree and now you're standing right there."

"A tree?" Zane said, in disbelief. "Did you ever hear of a ninja falling out of a tree before?"

"Well...no," Kruncha admitted.

"Then it doesn't make sense that one did tonight," said Zane. "Want to know what really happened?"

Kruncha nodded. Zane couldn't tell if the skeleton was

genuinely starting to disbelieve his own eyes or just waiting to see how far the ninja would push this, but he pressed on anyway.

"You were in your camp," said Zane. "Someone told you to go out and look for wood."

"Sure, Nuckal did," said Kruncha.

"Just before you left, Nuckal told you a joke," said Zane. "Ummmm . . . how did the ninja get up in the tree?"

Kruncha brightened. "I don't know, how?"

"He hid inside an acorn and let a squirrel carry him up," said Zane, doing his best to sound the way Jay did when he told a joke.

Kruncha laughed. "Ha! An acorn! Some big ninja hiding inside a little acorn ... that's a good one."

Zane took a step backwards. "Right. In fact, you were thinking about that joke the whole time you were walking here."

"I was?"

Zane took another step back. "Sure. Think about it – a little squirrel carrying a ninja up a tree. That's funny."

The ninja wasn't really sure if it was funny or not, but he had heard Cole tell the joke once and the others laughed. Kruncha certainly seemed to like it, as he started laughing even harder this time.

"So there you were, minding your own business, thinking about the joke, when you tripped and hit your, um, skull on a rock," Zane continued. "Naturally, you got all confused. When you got up, you thought you really were seeing a ninja who had been up in a tree. But, of course, you weren't."

"Right," said Kruncha. "Of course. That would be ridiculous. A ninja up a tree? You would have to be really stupid to believe that."

Zane took another step back. He was almost completely hidden by darkness now. "One more thing: I wouldn't tell anyone back at your camp about what you thought you saw. They wouldn't understand."

"Yeah, they wouldn't..." Kruncha began. But the ninja he had been talking to – well, the one he imagined he had been talking to – was gone.

Shrugging, the skeleton turned around and started picking up sticks to take back to camp. It had certainly been a strange night, but he was glad that the imaginary ninja had been nice enough to admit he wasn't real. It would have been embarrassing to tell Nuckal he had seen someone who clearly wasn't there.

* * *

Zane had gathered an armful of wood and was on his way back to camp. No doubt the others would be waiting for him. He looked forward to telling them about his adventure... and that, maybe, he finally got the joke.

Just Skulls and Dry Bones

Ninjas never underestimate their opponents ... even if they have no brains. Samukai's skeletons were dumb or crazy, but they came in their hundreds!

Krazi

Weapon of Choice: Bone
Elemental Colour: Blue
Strength: Speed

Krazi would pick a fight and flatten any form of life. No other skeleton is as wild, electric and supercharged with negative energy as Krazi. No other loves teasing rain clouds, either.

Chopov

Weapon of Choice: Machete
Elemental Colour: Black
Strength: Defence

Chopov is always ready to knock everything that would stand in his way off balance. Built like brick, he is as tough as a stone ... and twice as smart. No wonder he loves watching paint dry.

Frakjaw

Weapon of Choice: Mace Ball
Elemental Colour: Red
Strength: Attack

His burning anger makes his bones so hot and sizzling that wherever he appears he leaves a trail of ashes behind him. Frakjaw loves roasting marshmallows...stuck on the end of his spiky mace.

Bonezai

Weapon of Choice: Pickaxe
Elemental Colour: White
Strength: Stealth

Bonezai is very, very cold. His ice-cold-touch could freeze mortals together with their shadows in a split second. He is so cold that he even makes his favourite strawberry ice cream feel warm.

The Sensei asks

Even without brains or hearts, the skeletons had quite temperamental – or "elemental" – characters. What ninja elements would match each skeleton?

Answer: Krazi – Lightning, Chopov – Earth, Frakjaw – Fire, Bonezai – Ice.

The Ice Dragon

Searching for the golden Shurikens of Ice, my ninjas reached the distant and unwelcoming Frozen Wasteland. In a vast ice castle they found the weapon . . . and its mighty guardian.

The Ice Dragon was not entirely happy to see the intruders snatching the weapon from under his nose. It managed to freeze Zane together with the weapon he had grabbed into a solid block of ice.

The other three ninjas escaped the dragon's icy breath, carrying their frozen friend and the shurikens with them. At the time they didn't expect to see the Ice Dragon ever again . . . not to mention asking it for a favour.

It had to be something the Ice Dragon and Zane had in common that helped the two come to a quick agreement. With logical arguments Zane easily convinced the dragon to give him a ride to the realm of the skeletons.

Ninja Glossary
Part 2

Once you choose to follow the way of the ninjas, there is no going back. For once you start learning, you will want to learn more …

ashiaro – wooden pads carved to leave animal tracks, attached to the shoes to mislead the pursuit

bushi – a warrior

fukiya – a long blowgun, typically firing poison darts

hanbo – a three-foot long wooden staff

hitsuke – the practice of distracting guards by starting a fire away from the ninja's planned point of entry

jo – a four-foot wooden staff

katana-kaji – a swordsmith

makimono – the secret ninja scrolls held in a ryu

ninpo – the world view of the ninjas

nukenin – a ninja who left his village without authorisation and never returned

osa – a leader of the ninja village

ozutsu – cannons used to launch fiery sparks as well as projectiles at a target

ryu – a school of thought or a philosophy of a martial art style

tamahagane – a special combination of hard and tough types of steel, used for making swords

tanuki-gakure – the practice of climbing a tree and camouflaging oneself within the foliage

tessen – an iron fan used as a weapon

tsuba – a round or square hand guard on a sword

wakizashi – a short sword that can be hidden on the ninja's body

yogen – the knowledge of the mysterious powders, poisons, and potions used by ninjas

yumi – a Japanese longbow made of bamboo

廻転 Persevere 忍者 Ninja